BETRAYAL
Wrath of Karma

SHYAM SUNDAR BULUSU

DISCLAIMER

All the characters and situations portrayed in this story are fictitious. Any resemblance to situations and persons living or dead is purely coincidental.

To

My soul mate

Swarna

I miss **you**

Contents

Acknowledgements 9

Prologue 11

Kaveri's Journal - Entry #1 13

Shyam's Journal - The Only Entry 15

Kaveri's Journal - Entry #2 17

Kaveri's Journal - Entry #3 21

Kaveri's Journal - Entry #4 26

Kaveri's Journal - Entry #5 30

Kaveri's Journal - Entry #6 40

Kaveri's Journal - Entry #7 44

Kaveri's Journal - Entry #8 56

Kaveri's Journal - Entry #9 82

Shyam's Letter 96

Kaveri's Journal - Final Entry...............................99

Epilogue..101

Acknowledgements

I express my sincere gratitude to Notionpress, Chennai, for their unstinting help and guidance as also for providing an economical platform for launching my present work.

Writing a book may be easy but fine-tuning it, making it readable to international readers, and avoiding pedagogism and clichés are humongous tasks. In this aspect, I am lucky to have had the help of my nephew G. K. Srinivas, who is a staunch supporter as well as a bitter critic of my works. I cannot thank him enough for never mincing his words or opinions.

A special mention of the inspiration and support I received from my daughter, Sameera, throughout my escapades with words, will be in order. She patiently went through every single word of every book, every story, and every poem that I wrote, giving me constructive feedback on every facet, criticising when I erred, appreciating when I deserved

Shyam Sundar Bulusu

Prologue

What would you say if I told you that life served paradise on a silver platter to me and I let it slip through my fingers? Was it unbridled avarice, blind ambition, or implacable arrogance that made me trample upon those who loved me, who were dear to me?

I don't know. I don't have answers to any of these questions.

I am Kaveri and this is my story.

Kaveri's Journal - Entry #1

Shyam asked me with tears in his eyes why I was doing that to him, to us and if I did not love him. I told him that he misunderstood me and our relationship. *The fact, which I denied outwardly, was I loved him and had declared several times in the past that I loved him.* We were best friends right from our school days. During our college days, we declared our love for each other and decided that we would marry after we completed our education, got into employment, and when the time was right.

I broke up with him and dumped him.

Why did I do it?

My parents received an alliance proposal from an affluent family. Virendra had seen me at a friend's birthday party and liked me very much. My parents placed two options before me - marry Virendra and lead a comfortable and settled life or marry Shyam and struggle for the rest of my life even for basic things. Both Shyam and I came from lower middle-class families. I pictured a rosy life with Virendra as opposed to a lifelong struggle with Shyam. I did not waste any time on debating the issue. It is not as though I was married to Shyam. People break up and move on with their lives. It happens. It was as simple as that...*for me*.

What I didn't realise was the depth and intensity of Shyam's love for me.

That was about ten years ago. Shyam was out of my life completely.

Shyam's Journal - The Only Entry

Why have you done this to me, to us, Kavi? How am I going to live without you? I love you; I love you; I love you so much, Kavi, more than I love myself. Why Kavi, why?

Kavi

Kavi

Kavi

Kavi

Kavi

Kavi

Kavi

Today, you are becoming someone else's life-partner. My life has no meaning any longer. Why should I live? I am sorry, mom and dad; I love you. Please forgive me for what I am going to do.

Kaveri's Journal - Entry #2

Life is good. Viru and I had a great honeymoon in Europe. After we returned, life slowly fell into a routine. Viru was engrossed with his father in their business and was always busy. I finished a two-year course in fashion designing and planned to open my own fashion designing house. Viru and family, though initially reluctant, supported me and gave me all possible help; offered me financial assistance for launching my venture, which I declined. I wanted to do it under my own steam.

The family's reputation helped me in setting up my venture by way of finding a location for a large showroom and tailoring factory adjoining it in a prime business district. Securing a bank loan after investing my own substantial savings was hassle-free. I even borrowed heavily from a moneylender at a high rate of interest. Such was my passion for achieving my dream.

After three years of my marriage, I became the proud owner, nay *Proprietor*, of my fashion designing house with a showroom.

I named it *Kaveri Kreations - Fashion Designers.*

❧✳☙

Present day…

Kaveri briskly walked into the showroom, her stilettos clickety-clacking on the burgundy-coloured polished granite of the showroom floor, and reached her office chamber. The security guard had already kept the air-conditioners running. The entire office was cool, a great relief on another hot and sultry summer day.

'I'll talk to the manager first and then take a tour of the factory,' she thought. She started the desktop and soon lost herself in the labyrinth of endless emails.

❧✳☙

Kaveri found her manager, Santhana Krishnan, touching 60, standing anxiously in front of her. Looking at him quizzically, she motioned him to be seated.

'What now? He is getting nervous, easily ruffled nowadays.'

"Yes, Mr. Krishnan?"

"Ma'am, do you remember the order from *Kandan Art Pictures* for 200 battle costumes?"

"Hmmm…yes." Kaveri was well aware that number of drama companies and small-budget movie companies were their important customers; significant part of her company's economy and finances came from them. She was aiming to catch business from big movie houses, too.

"The date of delivery is two weeks from now."

"I'm aware of that, sir." Slightly annoyed.

"We took a substantial amount as advance. We are well into the designing part, too."

"Go on, sir, what are you getting at? Is there any problem? I thought things were running smoothly on that front!"

"They were, ma'am, they were, until now."

"So, what happened now?"

"The supplier of inner pads for the battle tunics has backed out."

"What? How?" Kaveri was shocked.

"Their manager called me this morning. Seems they are having some problems in their factory and won't be able to supply."

"What problems? How can he do this to us at the last minute? Have you explained to him the seriousness of the situation that we have a deadline to meet?"

"Yes, ma'am, I did. I spoke to him at length. He wouldn't budge."

"We don't have time to look for another supplier, Mr. Krishnan."

"No, ma'am, we don't. We shall need another two to three months for contracting another supplier, and for them to design and deliver our order."

"*Kandan Art Pictures* has deadlines, too, sir. They will not give us that length of time."

"What do we do now, ma'am?"

"Give me a few minutes and connect me to our supplier. I'll speak to him."

"Yes, ma'am."

❧❃❧

Kaveri's Journal - Entry #3

It proved to be a bad day, a very bad day. It happened suddenly, out of the blue. Not just the supplier, who was unrelenting, even the production manager of *Kandan Art Pictures*, our regular customers for years, was livid. He said he would get back to me after discussing the matter with his producers and director. He did. They cancelled their order and ordered me to return the advance amount within 48 hours. He said that the matter would not end there and that we would face consequences for our unprofessional behaviour, which had upset their production schedule resulting in losses. I tried beyond my best to explain the situation to him and begged him to relent. His final words were ominous, *'Be prepared to face the consequences for your betrayal of our trust in you.'*

I was not prepared for what happened next.

കൗ✳ൕ

Present day…

Kaveri looked up at Santhana Krishnan.

"What's up, Mr. Krishnan?"

"We have sent the cheque to *Kandan Art Pictures* by courier yesterday. They'd receive it today."

"Good."

"The advance amount, with interest on it, is large."

"I'm aware. We can't afford any more such hits, Mr. Krishnan. We have to be careful. Please keep a tight check on all orders in production stage. I'll monitor them personally."

"I'm on it."

"Don't be complacent."

❧❀❧

A week passed.

"Ma'am, Mr. Arunachalam from *Alpha Movies* has called. He wants you to call him immediately."

"OK, I will. What's the matter? Did he say anything? Give me an update on the status of their order before I call him."

જ*જ

"Hello, Mr. Arunachalam, how are you, sir? Our manager said you wanted me to call you."

"Yes."

"The heroine's costumes are in production stage. We will deliver it a few days before deadline. No worr…"

"There's a change of plans, Ms. Kaveri. We're cancelling the order."

"What? Why?"

"I am sorry, change in production plans."

"Mr. Arunachalam, you are saying this after we entered production stage, placed orders on subcontractors! We cannot cancel those orders, sir. We shall lose heavily. Why are you doing this, Mr. Arunachalam? We have been executing your orders to your full satisfaction for a few years now; never missed a deadline."

"Listen Ms. Kaveri. I cannot say anything more. Our order stands cancelled. We will give you two weeks to return the advance amount."

"Sir, this isn't fair. We'll lose heavily. We'll take recourse to legal action."

"Are you sure you want to do that? Read our contract terms carefully. You don't stand a chance against us. My advice is that you cut your losses and move on, and don't you ever issue threats, Ms. Kaveri. We don't take kindly to it."

"Sir…"

"One more thing, Ms. Kaveri, do not expect business from us anymore in future. Good bye."

സ✳സ

"What's happening, Mr. Krishnan, that is the second order that has been cancelled inside a week."

"I don't have a clue, ma'am…I'm shocked, too."

"The first one was a minor one; lost a few lakhs. We could have somehow withstood it, but the production manager of *Kandan Art Pictures* threatened me with *consequences*. The second case with the *Alpha Movies* was of disastrous proportions not only in terms of money but in terms of the reputation of our company."

"Yes, madam, I am afraid there may be consequences. I am worried about it. Word spreads very fast in their grapevines."

"The financial implications are very large. We will be in real trouble, sir."

Kaveri's Journal - Entry #4

My fears came true...about the *consequences*. The production manager must have spread word about our company.

The result...

...two projects, well into production stage, were cancelled, leaving us gasping for oxygen. The losses were over 50 lakh rupees; enormous for our small company, especially coming on the heels of the earlier two blows.

...four confirmed orders were cancelled, with a combined potential loss of business of over 30 lakh rupees.

...six more optimistic business deals under negotiation were called off.

We were only executing a couple of small orders, which were helping us keep our heads above water...just.

That, in a nutshell, was my previous month…an utter disaster.

What happened? I don't understand, just that our business is in soup.

Why has it happened? I absolutely have no clue.

I may have to resort to desperate measures to keep the business afloat…even laying off a few of the staff.

I was at my wit's end.

℘❀℘

A couple of months elapsed.

℘❀℘

Present day…

Santhana Krishnan was seated in front of Kaveri in her chamber. They were ruminating over the happenings of the previous months, not that they had much else to do.

"Ma'am, our finances are in bad shape…"

"I'm aware, Mr. Krishnan," replied Kaveri ruefully.

"I am not sure if we can even meet the staff salaries this month."

Kaveri's face was mirthless and grim.

"We may have to lay down some members of the staff, sir…with immediate effect."

"I am very sad it has come to this, ma'am."

"Me, too…didn't expect any such thing…at all. Come up with some proposals, Mr. Krishnan." Her voice was trembling when she said that.

❧❀❧

After a few more weeks…

Kaveri was sitting dejectedly in her chamber going through emails.

She buzzed her manager on the intercom.

"Mr. Krishnan, can you come to my chamber?"

A few minutes later Santhana Krishnan stood before Kaveri, who motioned him to sit.

"What are the updates, sir? Any business inquiries from anyone?"

"No, ma'am."

"What about our layoff plan? Have you issued termination orders to those ten employees?"

"Yes ma'am. It was a heart-breaking scene out there."

Tears welled in Kaveri's eyes.

"They have all worked so sincerely for me. What if they are the junior-most? How will they and their families cope? I feel guilty, sir."

"What else could you have done? You had no choice. We don't have funds to pay their salaries."

"Why doesn't that thought make me feel better?"

Santhana Krishnan maintained silence.

"Anything else, sir?"

"Nothing much, ma'am. A couple of inquiries came in in the last couple of days, nothing concrete. Nobody called back. I will follow up with them."

"Do that, please."

ೞ❀ೞ

Kaveri's Journal - Entry #5

That's it.

There are no fresh orders. Period.

It's over a month since we executed our last small order.

We are eating out of our reserve funds. They may not last long, surely not longer than a month or so.

Try as I might, I could not unravel the mystery of the sudden cancellation of orders. I even considered the conspiracy theory but brushed it away. We are not big players in the fashion designing market.

Everything was coming to an end. All my efforts, my struggles, my dedication, my passion had gone waste. I felt I might have to shut down my business completely. Or I can temporarily avoid shutting shop by laying off 50 per cent of the remaining staff. Either of the options was anathema to me.

So, over the months, I mortgaged my apartment and also took heavy loans at high interest rates from a loan shark. That has filled our coffers to some extent and gave us breathing time of a few months.

I did not have any other option.

ℭ❀ℭ

When Viru divorced me…

Yes, Viru and I divorced each other in the fourth year of our marriage.

When Viru divorced me, I got to keep our four-bedroom apartment and two luxury cars in addition to other one-time settlements. Our marriage turned so bitter that I did not want to have any monthly alimony factor. I wanted it done with.

The reasons for our divorce?

It's like in any other marriage, irreconcilable differences, incompatibility, and complete breakdown of our relationship. All that started soon after our honeymoon. It became worse day by day and ultimately ended in our decision to part ways permanently.

We divorced by mutual consent.

ભ❀ભ

During that period of turmoil, images from the happy times Shyam and I spent together used to flash briefly across my mind's eye in streams of consciousness. I used to brush them away as I did not want to add to my misery. In some remote corner of my mind, I used to feel a nagging sense of guilt.

Even after my divorce, I did not try to contact Shyam; I did not try to inquire about his and his family's welfare. I just wondered, *'How is he? Where is he? Is he married? Does he have children?'*

I immersed myself into my world of fashion designing and concentrated on consolidating my company's position in the market.

ભ❀ભ

Present day…

Following weeks saw many hits and misses by *Kaveri Kreations*. While there were some inquiries by potential customers, none materialised. Kaveri and Santhana Krishnan aggressively promoted the company in the market. They contacted many old customers but to no avail; it was as though entire film industry boycotted them.

Kaveri pacified Santhana Krishnan, "they say, it is the darkest before dawn. I agree these are difficult times but let's not lose hope. Let's keep going at it. Something somewhere has got to give in."

Santhana Krishnan nodded his head ruefully.

ക✳ക

Kaveri came out of her bathroom after a hot shower. She dried herself and got into pyjamas and tee shirt. She served herself a generous portion of the Chinese food she picked up on her way back home. She dumped herself in the sofa and turned on the giant-size TV.

Her cellphone rang.

ക✳ക

Kaveri rang her manager.

"Mr. Krishnan."

"Yes, ma'am."

"Sorry for calling so late. Hope I haven't disturbed your sleep."

"No, ma'am. It's OK."

"Just now I spoke with a Mr. Karan Malhotra, Senior Manager in *Shopping Bag*."

"They are online and brick-and-mortar retail chain of supermarkets giving stiff competition to other big players in the market. Right?"

"Yes, sir. Karan was talking about a big order…new designer uniforms for their counter salespersons and online home delivery partners."

Santhana Krishnan thought it better not to let hopes soar. After all, they were witnessing a near-massacre of their business.

"That would be a huge order, ma'am, if we can clinch it."

"Yes, sir…a few thousand designer uniforms, but let me…us…not get carried away in unbridled optimism. Caution is the key word."

"Yes."

"Can you come to the office a little early, say around 8 A.M.? Karan said he would visit our unit by about 8:30. I can fill you in before that."

"Sure, ma'am. I will be there."

"Good night, Mr. Krishnan."

"Good night, ma'am."

ೞ✤ೞ

Punctually at 8:30 A.M., Karan Malhotra walked into Kaveri's chamber and sat in front of her desk. He was about 30 years of age, about 5' 10", 65 kg, athletic in build, and smart.

"Good morning, Ms. Kaveri."

"Just Kaveri, sir."

"Ok. Karan for Kaveri."

She smiled and nodded. "He is Mr. Santhana Krishnan, our manager."

They sipped coffee and began the discussions.

ೞ✤ೞ

"Kaveri, you might be knowing about our organisation very well. We have over 100 outlets in Chennai itself and another 250 all over Tamil Nadu. We have plans to commence operations in entire south, but that is in the future. In Tamil Nadu, our employee strength is about 8000. The present uniforms of various categories of employees have been in force right from inception. We have decided to revamp the uniforms for different categories according to present-day requirements and contemporary aesthetic styles. We plan to provide three sets of uniforms for each employee as also maintain reserves. There must be a scope for repeat orders, too. So, you can imagine the numbers involved."

"I am aware that you are a fashion designing graduate. Our MD and I have seen your work. It is impressive. We would like to assign the project to your firm if we reach an agreement. You will be required to submit a few designs for each category for our approval. We may have suggestions, too. I am available for discussions, should the need arise. The project should be completed in three months. We would like to launch the new uniforms on Pongal day. The deadline is non-negotiable.

"Now, I'd like to visit your factory."

❧✿❧

"There are less than 20 tailoring personnel, Kaveri!"

"Karan, to tell the truth, our business has suffered terrible losses in recent months. Keeping it afloat was possible only if we laid off a substantial number of workers."

"How are you going to execute an order this big within the deadline with this staff?"

"No worries, Karan, we can rehire them and hire more if needed. We can work overtime and offer target-oriented incentives."

"OK. We would like to see the staff in full strength within a few days of our confirmation."

"Sure, Karan."

"So, I shall apprise our MD of all details and communicate his decision soon."

"Thanks, Karan."

They shook hands and Karan Malhotra left for his office.

Santhana Krishnan could see a faint glow of hope emerge in Kaveri's despondent eyes.

☙❋❧

They had to wait for two days to receive any communication from Karan, but they dare not contact him themselves. On the third day, the suspense ended when Kaveri received a fax from Karan confirming their order. Over the next few days, Kaveri, Santhana Krishnan, and employees from administration and account departments worked day and night and sent appointment letters to over thirty tailoring technicians, some of whom were laid off in the previous weeks. The tailoring factory staff strength looked healthy at over 50.

Kaveri Kreations was once again raring to go.

☙❋❧

The following days saw Kaveri holding extensive discussions with Karan on the designs of uniforms for each category of employees. She worked day and night on creating several design options. She submitted her proposals – multiple designs for each category – to Karan, who promised to get back to her within two days and he did.

Armed with the approved designs, Kaveri created the meticulously and precisely crafted prototypes of the designs. Then again, she invited Karan to visit and inspect them *in situ*, which he did.

"What about your MD? Doesn't he have to inspect them before we enter production?"

"He is an extremely busy man. Won't be able to spare time, especially with our expansion plans moving ahead swiftly. Don't worry. I'll brief him and convey his approval in a day or two, max. OK?"

Kaveri smiled and nodded.

Kaveri's Journal - Entry #6

Things seem to have started looking up again for my *Kaveri Kreations.* I must be cautiously optimistic about it. What do they say...*once bitten... twice shy*? Contract was signed. Final, category-wise designs were approved. We rolled into production stage smoothly. I wanted to meet with the MD of *Shopping Bag* but couldn't; it seemed he was very busy. Some other time, perhaps.

The collective sound of over 50 sewing machines was like sweet music to the ears. A feeling of euphoria was slowly settling in.

೮ଃ✲೮ଃ

The euphoria was too good to last.

೮ଃ✲೮ଃ

Present day...

Navratri came and went. *Kaveri Kreations* celebrated it with enthusiasm as they did every year. Then came

Deepavali, bringing with it the sound of firecrackers and the glow of hundreds of lamps.

The short-time targets were being met with no hiccups. Monitoring the progress carefully and strictly, Kaveri fine-tuned the work wherever necessary.

She was reporting periodically to Karan about the progress being made. He seemed satisfied. Kaveri felt that her dream company was, finally, out of the woods. She was feeling very happy...

...until two lightning bolts struck her...

৩❀৩

Kaveri received two phone calls that day. Both were similar in nature. Both sounded the death knell to her. She sat petrified in her chair, not understanding what had just happened, not knowing what to do.

She summoned her manager into the chamber.

৩❀৩

"You know that I had borrowed heavily from the private bank as also from a loan shark for starting *Kaveri Kreations,* don't you?"

"Yes, I do."

"The bank has given me two weeks' time to repay the mortgage amount we got from them failing which my business will be taken over by them. It is over one crore rupees, sir."

Before Santhana Krishnan could respond, Kaveri continued.

"The loan shark was threatening of dire consequences if we do not return his loan amount within a week. It is 50 lakh rupees. Wherefrom will I get such a huge amount in a week, Mr. Krishnan?"

"Did you find out why they are doing it all of a sudden? Haven't you been paying interest amounts regularly?"

"No, I have defaulted for several months. I tried to plead with them but to no avail, especially the loan shark. The private bank was no better but they were at least courteous; not that courtesy helps."

"So, what do you plan to do, ma'am? Can we approach *Shopping Bag* for another advance?"

"Absolutely not. If they get a whiff of what's going on, they'll just cancel the order; we'll be finished."

She was lost in thought for a couple of minutes.

"Mr. Krishnan, don't worry. I'll think of something. Just go on with the work as per schedule; no slip-ups there."

Santhana Krishnan nodded and left her chamber.

Kaveri's Journal - Entry #7

I am sure someone has cast an evil eye on my *Kaveri Kreations*. Otherwise, how do I explain what's going on - one trouble after another. This is the worst of all; if I don't find a solution immediately this would be the end of my dream.

Let me think...let me think...let me think...

☙❈❧

Present day...

"Are you sure, Kaveri ma'am? That's a very serious thing."

"I thought about it a lot. There is no other option to tide over this crisis. In about a month, we have to deliver the order and then get paid. Things will be better after that. So..."

"You are talking of selling your apartment to the loan shark, ma'am!"

"To pay off the 50-lakh-rupee debt. I expect 2.5-3.0 crore rupees from the sale. It will leave about 2 crore rupees in the reserve for our company. Even if we pay off interest amount to the bank it will leave enough reserves for us until we deliver the order. Right?"

"I don't know. It all seems quite complicated and… risky."

"Don't worry, I've got it all covered."

ೞ✿ೞ

Kaveri had no idea about the rude shock she was about to receive.

ೞ✿ೞ

There was a smallish-looking man in white *veshti* and green tee shirt sitting behind a medium-size table. He had a laptop open in front of him. There were two old, large steel cupboards behind him against the wall. A ceiling fan was working overtime to provide a semblance of breeze inside the dingy room lit by couple of LED tube lights. He was speaking on his cellphone with someone and motioned Kaveri to sit in front of him.

Nothing about him or the room gave away the fact that the person, in front of whom Kaveri was sitting, was the dreaded loan shark Karuppayya. He seemed quite religious with three bands of *vibhuti* and *a kumkum* dot on his forehead.

"What have you decided, madam?" Karuppayya's voice was almost courteous.

"Sir, I don't have that kind of money readily available. Will you please give me a few more months? I am finishing work on an order. It must be delivered before *Pongal*. I will receive payment for that shortly afterwards. Please."

He looked at her hawk-like eyes. "Madam, I am not in the charity business. I must serve other customers also. I must roll my money. So, my answer is 'no'. Either pay up by tomorrow or face consequences." His tone turned menacing.

Kaveri looked crestfallen. Karuppayya was not interested in the least bit. Finally, she made her proposal of selling her apartment. The haggling went on for a long time. Karuppayya rejected her demand of three crore rupees and finally, offered her one crore sixty lakh rupees from which, his earlier loan of fifty lakh rupees would be deducted with interest.

'Beggars are not choosers and I am the beggar now. This or lose the business altogether,' she thought.

"Yes, sir. I agree."

"OK, madam, you send me copies of all the originals on *WhatsApp* by tonight. I shall get the sale papers ready by tomorrow. You come back at the same time tomorrow evening for signatures. You can bring your own witness. I shall have one of my own."

"OK, sir." Her heart was heavy. She suppressed her tears of loss and humiliation and stood up to leave.

Indifferent to her presence, Karuppayya began speaking to someone over his cellphone.

ᏣᏣ❋ᏣᏣ

The next few days saw the transfer of ownership of Kaveri's apartment to Karuppayya. True to his word, Karuppayya made full payment after deducting the loan given to Kaveri along with interest upon that. He permitted her to stay on for one month for making alternate arrangements. A deeply saddened and depressed Kaveri collected the cash and returned home.

಍❀಍

While one issue was resolved, the other one was hanging on her head like the sword of Damocles... the loan she took from a private bank.

Kaveri was extremely worried.

಍❀಍

Kaveri was extremely worried as she entered the chamber of the bank Manager, Mr. Unni Nambiar.

Pleasantries were exchanged.

"I'll come straight to the point, Ms. Kaveri. It has been several months. Your company has been in default in paying the monthly interest. We have reminded through emails, text messages, and phone calls. You always offer excuses for not paying...cancellation of orders, financial problems and the like."

"I am sorry for the delay, Mr. Nambiar but the reasons are true. We are passing through a very difficult period..."

"I'm sorry, but how does that concern us, Ms. Kaveri?"

"Sir, I beg you. Please try to understand. We are executing a big order, which must be delivered before *Pongal.* After that, we will receive our payment and I will clear all the arrears to your bank."

"No, ma'am, not acceptable. You are in breach of the loan agreement. I tried to shield you from my higher authorities for as long as I could. You see, we are in business, too, and we are facing serious money crunch after the pandemic. We even had to shut down some branches and lay off some staff. So, *you* try to understand *our* problem. Our HQ has already made a decision. They will proceed strictly in accordance with the terms and conditions of the agreement. They will be initiating legal process to confiscate and seize your company."

Kaveri was in tears. Her voice was a choked whisper when she said, "Sir…"

"I'm sorry, Ms. Kaveri, it had to come to this. It's upon you. Have a good day."

Tears streaming down her cheeks, Kaveri ran out of the chamber and the building.

જ*જ

Next morning...

Kaveri just finished a conversation with her lawyer over phone.

She heard a soft knock on the glass door.

"Come in, Mr. Krishnan."

Santhana Krishnan was fidgety in his chair.

'Now what?' thought Kaveri. She narrated to him the details of previous day's discussions with Mr. Nambiar.

"Ma'am, the situation is not good, not good at all."

"Yes, I know but is there a way out? Do you have any suggestions?"

"I already suggested, ma'am, but you rejected it."

"That I should approach Karan Malhotra for another advance?"

Santhana Krishnan nodded.

"Do you realise what will happen? He will cancel the order immediately."

"Maybe he will, maybe he won't, but the other option of *not doing anything* is certainly curtains for *Kaveri Kreations*."

Kaveri fell silent. The tension in the room was palpable. Santhana Krishnan slowly placed an envelope on the table.

"What is this, sir?"

Santhana Krishnan seemed to hesitate for a few moments. Then he spoke.

"My resignation, ma'am."

Kaveri could not believe her ears. "What?"

Santhana Krishnan did not respond.

"You, too, Mr. Krishnan?"

He maintained complete silence.

"Now, of all times!" Kaveri exclaimed in pain.

He cleared his throat and said, "Ma'am, what choice do I have? I don't know how many days this business house is going to survive. You don't have even enough funds to pay the monthly instalment to the bank. The bank has already initiated legal action. I have a family to support and my wife is under medical treatment. Where will I go if I don't have a job and a regular income?"

"I understand, Mr. Krishnan, but of all the times, now! Things will improve, sir. I'll think of something..."

He interrupted her. "What and how?"

She had no answer.

"You don't even want to try to talk with Karan..."

"OK. I agree. I should have talked to him a couple of days earlier. I'll try now. Until then, can you wait? Please?"

"OK, ma'am." He picked up his envelope and left.

ఆ❈ఆ

Kaveri was chaperoned into Karan Malhotra's chamber by the security staff. Karan looked up from some papers, welcomed her, and motioned her to be seated. Kaveri sat in a comfortable chair and adjusted her dress.

"Yes, Kaveri, what can I do for you?" Karan said with a smile.

Kaveri recounted in detail the events of the previous few days – the severe paucity of funds, her selling the apartment, and the bank mortgage issue.

For the next few minutes, they sat silently sipping their coffee. Finally, Karan broke the silence and spoke in a sympathetic tone.

"I am extremely sorry for what you are going through, Kaveri. What can I do for you?"

She spoke at length about the financial mess her company had been passing through over the past few months – the cancellation of orders and other setbacks. She requested him to help her by giving her company a further advance to cover the bank's overdue EMI.

"If I cannot solve this within a day or two, at best, I'll lose the company. The bank is moving legal channels and I am likely to get their notice within two or three days."

Karan fell silent for a few minutes.

"Kaveri, this matter cannot be decided upon by me. I'll have to escalate it to our MD. The amount you require isn't a small one; we have already given an advance *vis-à-vis* our order. This is your company's establishment matter; doesn't concern us. I'll inform our MD and let him decide."

⁂

Forty-eight hours later, Kaveri's world imploded.

⁂

Karan conveyed his MD's inability to offer further advance on their order and told her to adhere to the delivery deadline strictly.

⁂

The bank issued a legal notice to Kaveri, thus initiating the legal process of seizing *Kaveri Kreations* for continued and prolonged failure to pay the overdue EMIs or the interest thereon.

⁂

Santhana Krishnan, the Manager of *Kaveri Kreations*, submitted his resignation and quit.

⁂

Sensing the serious existential crisis of *Kaveri Kreations*, a major chunk of the staff quit with immediate effect.

Kaveri's Journal - Entry #8

My dream has imploded.

Over six months elapsed…

Present day…

The case went to court. Based on the evidence submitted by the bank, the court found it to be an open-and-shut case and delivered its verdict in favour of the bank.

The bank held the company as a defaulted asset and advertised in the market for its sale.

Losing her own apartment and business, Kaveri had nowhere to live. She accepted her parents' offer to live with them until she sorted out her life.

The ringing of her cellphone woke Kaveri up from her disturbed sleep. She opened her eyes a crack and looked at the LED screen. The call was from Karan Malhotra. She cut the call and tried to go back to sleep. The calls from Karan kept coming and Kaveri kept cutting them. After a while, she received a text message.

"Hi K.

Tried calling many times. You've cut the calls. Need to speak urgently. Call when free. Good day.

K."

❧❋❧

After much thought, Kaveri called Karan.

"Kaveri, this is Karan."

"I know. What do you want?" She asked brusquely. Soft chuckle. "Ouch…Looks like someone is still angry…"

"Cut the bullshit, Karan. Come to the point." She snapped.

"OK, OK."

"What do you want? Haven't you done enough?"

There was silence for a few moments.

"I understand your anger but it is business, you see, unable to provide a loan, loss of our order…We have lost, too, if you care to know."

"Oh, I am sorry; my heart bleeds for your loss, Karan. I'm not interested in this bullshit. Why were you calling me? To offer your condolences? I heard that your *Shopping Bag* has purchased *Kaveri Kreations* from the bank?"

"You heard wrongly. *Shopping Bag* hasn't taken over your *Kaveri Kreations*. It was…" Karan paused. "I can't make you understand. So, I'll come to the point."

"Thank God. At last…"

"Do you want to understand your situation, to know why things went wrong with you?"

Kaveri was puzzled.

"What are you talking about?" Her suspicion and distrust were palpable.

"Go to the address that I'll give you and ask to meet with their top boss."

"Is this a trap? I don't have another *Kaveri Kreations* to offer to you."

"Your sarcasm doesn't bother me the least bit, Kaveri. Jot down this address…" Karan gave an address, which Kaveri scribbled on a post-it notepad. "Give them your name. Ask to meet with the top boss. You will understand everything."

"No name or phone number?"

"Just go to the address, Kaveri. Bye."

ରେ❋ରେ

The next day…

Kaveri parked her car in the parking lot of the four-storey edifice, which bore the name *Kamakshi Finserv* at the top. She slowly walked into the foyer, her stilettos clickety-clacking on the polished granite floor. The foyer was buzzing with activity of people scurrying across the floor. Some were waiting near the elevators and a few more were talking to the receptionist. Kaveri adjusted her leather handbag on her shoulder and walked to the receptionist. She waited for her turn and spoke to the receptionist.

"How can I help you, ma'am?" The receptionist's voice was well-trained, soft, and courteous.

"My name is Kaveri. I have to see…"

The receptionist interrupted politely. "Good morning, Kaveri ma'am. Will you please take the lift and go to the top floor?" She waved to a housekeeping worker busy mopping the floor and said to her, "Sarala, will you please take this madam in the private elevator to sir's chamber?"

Kaveri was intrigued. *'Was she expecting me?'*

Sarala guided Kaveri into an elevator with the inscription *'PRIVATE'* on its door. Shortly, Kaveri was sitting opposite a large mahogany desk in a large glass-walled chamber.

❧❀❧

Everything about the chamber was elegant; pastel hues for curtains and upholstery, soft-curved wooden furniture, and no garish decoration. The entire ensemble was very soothing and easy on the eye. She felt a calming effect on her disturbed mind.

❧❀❧

Sitting cross-legged, Kaveri was going through a colourful magazine on finance and commerce. She heard a soft whirring sound and turned towards the door. An electrical wheelchair was entering the chamber. It was carrying...

Her jaw dropped an inch. She blurted out one single word, a name, "Shyam!"

❧❀❧

"Yes, Mrs. Kaveri."

The same soft but firm voice. The same lean figure. Ten years had added a little grey in the hair and the hairstyle was short, close-cropped. The addition to the facial ensemble was a pair of thin-frame spectacles. He looked weak and tired. None of these aspects of Shyam shocked Kaveri. The one aspect that shocked her speechless was...

Shyam was ambulating in a wheelchair!

❧❀❧

"Shyam!" Kaveri repeated in surprise.

There was no smile on his face when he nodded and reached behind the desk.

"What is with the wheelchair?" The tremble in her voice was a dead giveaway of her concern.

Shyam just waved away the question and asked, "Will you have coffee, tea, or cold drink?"

His brusqueness offended her but she did not show it.

"Coffee will do; with milk and two sugars."

Shyam gave suitable instructions to Sarala, who respectfully withdrew from the chamber.

"How are you, Shyam?"

Again, his response was brusque.

"How can I help you?"

Once again, Kaveri let it pass.

"Karan asked me to go to this address and ask for the top boss. He didn't mention it was you."

"I told him not to."

"He also said if I wanted to understand why things went wrong with me and my business, I should get the answers here."

"He was under instructions."

"*Your*…instructions?"

"Yes."

"All right. Tell me."

"Not so fast, Mrs. Kaveri…"

"You can call me Kaveri or Kavi."

"Sorry, that's not going to happen."

She was hurt, but she said, "OK."

"As I said, not so fast, let's first have coffee. I have some urgent work for about half an hour. If you can wait, I'll finish it and then we can leave."

"Leave? Whereto?"

"You'll see, unless you have an objection."

Kaveri thought for a few seconds.

"It's ok. I'll wait."

❧✳❧

Coffee came on a trolley pushed by a short, slim girl in dark grey skirt and white tops.

"Give me fifteen minutes, Sarah, and I shall dictate some letters."

"OK, Shyam." She withdrew from the chamber.

Kaveri was surprised by the informal way of addressing the boss. They sipped the coffee in silence.

"Karan said it wasn't the *Shopping Bag* that acquired *Kaveri Kreations* from the bank."

"He is right; it wasn't."

"Then...who?"

"*Kamakshi Finserv.*"

"*Kamakshi Finserv?* The financial services and consultancy organisation?"

"Yes."

"I vaguely know they are a big name in the field but how are they involved in fashion designing?"

"They are not."

"Then, how come they..."

Shyam interrupted her.

"Kamakshi is my mother's name. I own Kamakshi Finserv." Kaveri was speechless.

಄✻಄

Kaveri wanted to know why it all happened to her and her dream project. Shyam insisted that it was not the place to discuss personal matters. He said that they should go to an appropriate place for that.

"Where?" She asked.

"Where it all began," he replied cryptically.

಄✻಄

He led her to what was, in good old times, their favourite niche, their favourite cement bench behind some bushes in the park near their homes. Kaveri was visibly nervous and anxious. She had not visited the park since she married Virendra.

"Why here, Shyam? Why not some 5-star hotel dining place? Or your home or mine?"

"Are you nervous?"

Her furtive looks said enough.

"Nostalgia is one reason and poetic justice is another. Please sit." He motioned her towards the bench. She silently complied. Shyam positioned his wheelchair a few feet away from her. Adjusting her dress, she sat stiffly on the bench and looked at him.

"So, you took over my company!"

"Yes."

"You shattered the dream of my life." There was nothing but contempt in her tone.

"Yes."

"Why?" She screamed.

He was silent for a few moments. She was observing him closely, anger and hatred spilling out of her eyes. Suddenly, she realised that his demeanour started to change. His looks became piercing and vicious. A reddish hue filled his eyes. Then he spoke slowly, steadily, and extremely deliberately. His eyes were brimming with implacable viciousness.

"I vowed to destroy you completely."

"Wh…What?" She was trembling.

"For your betrayal. For spitting on my love. For breaching my trust. For humiliating me with cruel words. For what it all did to my family."

She could not believe what she heard. She stared at him in wide-eyed horror.

"As you sow so shall you reap. Remember?"

"What? Nonsense. What have I sown that I should receive this?"

"You want to play it that way? All right."

"Are you referring to our breakup?"

Shyam was silent.

"Are you?" She repeated angrily.

"It was not merely a breakup; it was unashamed betrayal."

He paused for a few moments and continued.

"You are wailing about *your* dreams! *You* destroyed *my* dreams, *our* dreams. Not only dreams, you effectively destroyed my life."

"Oh God, the sentimentalist. Now, don't start crying," she mocked.

Shyam smiled.

"Is something funny?" She snapped.

"Yes, you."

"What?"

"Why are you sentimental about *your* dream… what's it you call it, *Kaveri Kreations*? Why are *you* crying? It's just business and you lost it. So what?"

"You bastard, it is my life's dream." She screamed and started crying.

Shyam made no move to console her.

"You deserved it for what you did to me."

She lifted her face from her palms and looked at him in seething anger.

"How dare you…"

"Oh, shut up. Stop being self-righteous, after you destroyed my life." He paused. "You asked me what was with the wheelchair, right?"

She wiped her tears and looked at him quizzically and nodded.

"I'll show you something and then tell you a story… of betrayal, breach of love and trust."

He loosened his necktie and opened the top couple of buttons of his shirt. There it was, nesting behind the buttoned-up collar and the necktie, *an ugly welt on the throat.*

"Oh my God, what is it?"

"Scar...left by a nylon clothes rope."

"What? What was a rope doing...? Oh God! You didn't, did you?"

Shyam responded calmly.

"I hanged myself from the ceiling fan with a nylon rope."

Kaveri was speechless and was gasping.

"It was about ten years ago. After we talked right here, you left after humiliating me, mocking me and my family, and calling me names. You spat on our love of years, from our college days. You lied that you didn't love me and that I misunderstood your friendship. You betrayed me for money and a luxurious life, for a greener pasture."

"To say that I was devastated would be an understatement. I was effectively and completely destroyed. I sat here long after you dumped me. I didn't know what to do or whom to talk with. My mind jammed up. That night, I slept here, on this bench. When I didn't return home even late in the night my parents panicked. Dad called me. I told him where I was. At about 2 o'clock in the night, he came looking for me. I didn't want to go home. I told him what happened and we spoke at length. He cajoled me for a long time and took me home. I went straight to my room and shut the door. Mom knocked several times but I didn't respond. Dad explained to her the situation. They were devastated, too. You weren't just a friend's daughter; you were family to us. They couldn't believe it.

"The next 10 days until your wedding were hell on earth for me. I just locked myself up in my room; came out only for food, that too upon mom's insistence. I stopped going out, watching TV, taking calls from friends. Day after day, I used to shed tears silently, looking at our photos and listening to your old voice messages.

"Finally, it was your wedding day. I realised that, on that day, I would lose you forever and from that day you would be someone else's. I died that day. My life lost all its meaning and purpose. I didn't merely love you like in *'I love you'*. *I loved you so much that*

I never saw my very existence beyond you. When you left me, I became empty. On your wedding day, I lost everything in the world. I didn't know why I should continue to live. I took a plastic clothes rope and hanged myself from the ceiling fan. The noose tightened around my neck and choked me. I wasn't able to breathe and was flailing my feet. I don't know what happened next. After a minute or so, I blacked out."

Shyam paused for breath. He buttoned up his shirt collar and adjusted the necktie. Kaveri's tears wouldn't stop. She listened to him in open-mouthed horror.

"Later, dad told me that I didn't come out for food and I didn't respond to his or mom's call. They knocked for long minutes. With the help of our neighbours they broke open the door. They found me dangling from the ceiling fan. I was unconscious. There was no pulse. I wasn't breathing. Someone called for an ambulance and took me to a hospital. I was alive, barely. I remained in coma for four days, it seems. The doctors saved me after Herculean efforts. I regained consciousness on the fourth day.

"When I came to, I didn't find dad or mom at the hospital. I was surprised. An uncle of mine was around. He gave me the deadliest news of my life. Seeing me hanging from the ceiling fan and also in coma at the hospital was too much for my mom. She had a massive heart attack the next day and died before she could be brought to the hospital."

Shyam paused again and wiped his tears. However, Kaveri's situation was a different story. She was overwhelmed by a sense of guilt and was openly sobbing in grief. She was very fond of Shyam's parents and they treated her like a daughter they never had. They doted on her showering her with their love, her favourite food, and gifts.

"I am sorry, aunty...I am sorry..."

Shyam didn't make any sort of move to console her. His disgust for her resurfaced redoubled.

From behind her hands covering her face, she spoke in a hoarse whisper.

"I'm sorry, Shyam. I didn't know any of this."

Shyam cut her short.

"Why would you? You made yourself clear that evening - what you felt about us..."

She interrupted him.

"You could have told me...at least afterwards."

"Why? You dumped me and we were no longer part of your life."

"I loved them, Shyam."

"It didn't sound like it that evening, Mrs. Kaveri, and if you really cared for them, as you claim, why didn't you visit them in the last ten years?"

She had no answer. There was silence for a few moments.

"What's with the...wheelchair..." She repeated.

"Doctors said that my cervical spine was badly damaged when I hanged myself. There was also some brain damage due to cut-off of oxygen to the brain. I used to get bouts of giddiness. I started using a walking stick for support and balance. Once, I fainted and fell off the staircase and severely damaged my lower spine, too. This paralysed me waist below. Then onwards, I started my journey in a wheelchair."

She was staring at him with tear-filled eyes. She stretched her right hand and tried to touch him on the cheek. Shyam pushed her hand away.

"My father, despite his own terrible personal loss, took care of me … like I was a baby…I literally was… from feeding, brushing and bathing me…even my toilet needs. To add to the boiling cauldron of problems, he had to keep me afloat from the abyss of my depression caused by your betrayal, mom's demise, and my own health issues. He was there for me, with me every moment. If I survived and am almost normal it was due to him."

He paused and took deep breath.

"How is uncle? How is he taking all this?"

Shyam took his time in responding. He gave her a wry smile.

"Two years after mom died, he was diagnosed with leukaemia…in the final stages. In taking care of me and helping me with my business venture, he utterly neglected his own health. When leukaemia was diagnosed it was already too late for him. His last few months were terrible. I felt relieved for him when he passed. One silver lining was he could see *Kamakshi Finserv* begin functioning; in fact, he inaugurated it." Shyam wiped his tears. "I miss him badly. From then on, it was I and my wheelchair."

Kaveri broke down completely. She fell on her knees and covered her face crying uncontrollably.

"I am sorry, uncle. I am sorry, aunty…"

"What is the point in all this now?"

"I am sorry…"

"Are you?"

Kaveri kept sobbing.

"We don't understand the pain of losing someone or something near and dear until it happens to us. You didn't, until you lost your home and your dream."

Shyam moved his wheelchair couple of feet away from her and continued to speak.

"For long months, I was lost in pain, sorrow, and depression. I tried to understand the whys and hows of what had happened. My life ended here, at this very spot. Your betrayal destroyed me and sent me plummeting into a dark abyss. It caused my suicide attempt and my mom's death. It shattered my family completely. I lost my best friend, my father. Ending up in this wheelchair is the nadir of my life."

"Mrs. Kaveri, *you* completely ruined my life. You betrayed my love, my trust. You took away my life. You destroyed my dream of a loving family with you and our children. I vowed that I would destroy your life, your dream; that I would take away everything that you loved.

"I picked myself up from the ashes, literally. For the next couple of years, I worked ceaselessly, day and night to build my venture, *Kamakshi Finserv,* into one of the top organisations in the field. I succeeded. I diversified into some other small ventures and consolidated them. Another feather in my cap was starting *Shopping Bag.* Finally, dame luck smiled on me most benevolently. *Shopping Bag* also became one of the top organisations in its field.

"While I was building my world, *I didn't forget you; I kept close watch on you*, your personal life, and your business. You know, *karma* always comes back. You do good to others; it will reward you. You harm someone; it'll punish you, sooner or later. You ruined the life of my loving family. We loved you wholeheartedly. I loved you more than I loved myself. Your *karma* started coming back at you. The first sign was your divorce from Virendra, for whom you dumped me most brazenly. You didn't live with him happily even for two years.

"Mrs. Kaveri, ambition itself is not bad, but when it harms or destroys someone, especially someone who loves you so much, *karma* comes back at you with brutal force and in ways you can't even imagine; *it came back at you in my form*.

"Yes, I am your *karma*. I engineered every debacle of yours, the cancelled orders, the squeezed supplies, the tightening of screws by the moneylender and the consequent loss of your house, the bank-loan fiasco and the resulting loss of your dream *Kaveri Kreations*. Now, you live with your parents. You don't have a job. You are thirty-five, divorced, and childless. You are goalless and rudderless. Yes, I engineered your downfall and brought you to your knees, just like what you did to me ten years ago. Still, I'd say you are in a better condition since you haven't experienced the loss of dear parents and a failed suicide attempt." He paused for breath. *"How does it feel, Mrs. Kaveri?"*

⁊❋⁊

"How does it feel, Mrs. Kaveri?"

A torrent of tears rolled down Kaveri's cheeks. She screamed. Her eyes were bloodshot. Her face was kohl-smeared. The *dupatta* on her chest was wet with her tears. It would be a heart-rending picture to others, *but not to Shyam.*

"Why? Why did you do it?"

Shyam looked at her in contempt but remained silent, his eyes glowering.

"Why, Shyam?"

"You know very well, Mrs. Kaveri. Look at me. What do I have to live for? For whom must I live?"

"Is it vendetta, revenge?"

"Call it whatever you want to; it doesn't matter. I'll ask you the same question as you asked me. I asked it ten years ago, too? Why did you do it to me?"

"Is it wrong to have a dream of my own?"

"I told you; dream or ambition itself is not bad, but it is when it harms someone. Me? I was not merely *harmed*; I was completely destroyed. I have nothing to live for. I needed to teach you a lesson for what you had done. I wanted to give you another chance. Remember, how many times I called you, texted you until your wedding day?"

"I was getting married to someone else, Shyam; we were finished; we broke up. There was no going back...at least for me."

"*We* didn't break up, Mrs. Kaveri; you broke up our relation, our love, due to your avarice, arrogance, and ambition. You wanted to rise in life *at any cost*; even if it meant trampling upon your near and dear and loved ones. *Look at you! Even now you haven't realised the enormity of what you had done to me and my family*. That was the kind of intoxication the greener pasture had on you. You didn't mind destroying me, my mother and father, and my life.

"Ultimately, what happened to your life? Where is your dream? Where is your much-flaunted marriage? Where is your home-sweet-home? You don't even have any children. You are at the nadir of your life."

He paused for a few moments and took deep breaths. Kaveri wiped the wetness on her cheeks as best as she could.

"Now what, Shyam?"

"I don't know and I don't care. I couldn't let your betrayal go unpunished. I did what I had to do. I am finished. I have a life – or what's left of it - to live until my end comes."

There were several long minutes of silence. Then he pulled out his cellphone and called his driver. The driver came within a couple of minutes to take Shyam to their car.

In a calm tone Shyam said, "Good bye, Mrs. Kaveri."

"Can I visit your home, Shyam, just for a few minutes, to see the pictures of uncle and aunty?" Tears were streaming down her cheeks once again.

Shyam calmly asked, "What for, Mrs. Kaveri? *You and I are finished; please realise that.*"

As Kaveri watched with tear-filled eyes, the driver pushed the wheelchair to the park gates. Moments later, the car disappeared from her sight.

Kaveri kept staring at the emptiness in front of her and inside of her.

Kaveri's Journal - Entry #9

What can I say?

Never in my life was I shocked more than I was that evening.

I have been thinking a lot about what Shyam said that evening. He has always been a very gentle person, especially towards me. That he turned so... vengeful and unforgiving...speaks volumes about what caused him to morph so. I was too busy with my venture to realise it until Shyam pointed out to me.

I am guilty...of the most shameless betrayal. I realise that *now*. I was so shocked about it all...Shyam, aunty, and uncle...that I didn't utter even a singe word of apology to him; not that it would *undo* the tragedy but that it would mean admission of guilt. I will meet with him again, if he will, and tender an unconditional apology; doesn't matter even if he won't accept it.

Seeing Shyam after ten years, especially in that condition, churned my stomach. Shyam in a *wheelchair*? I can't digest it. Yet, it is true. I cannot openly say *'my Shyam'* but I can say that in private to you, can't I?

My Shyam ambulates in a wheelchair! He attempted suicide and almost died! Aunty is dead. Uncle is dead. All because of me! Shyam says so; not directly but indirectly, as side effects to what I did to my Shyam ten years ago. I am responsible. That was my own family. They treated me as their own and what did I do? If that one evening is erased none of these tragedies would have happened. Shyam and I would be married now and would be having two or three children. Knowing how hardworking he is, I have no doubt about his success and I would be part of it all now.

But it wasn't to be. I had to choose the greener pasture, which proved to be not so green, after all. Of course, that was in may favour, too; I got the apartment, the cars, and the start-up, right? The question is, *'At what cost?'* My blind ambition, nay avarice, alienated and antagonised the one person, who loved me more than he did himself.

Oh God, what have I done!

I feel I would have done the exact same thing to him if he had betrayed me in a similar way, *but he would do no such thing, would he*? So, I feel I deserved what I got.

Karma always comes back, doesn't it?

಄❀಄

Present day…

Kaveri was busy preparing breakfast on a Sunday morning when her cellphone rang. It was from Karan.

'Why is he calling?' She was annoyed.

She answered the call.

"Hello."

"Hello, Kaveri, this is Karan. Good morning."

"I know. Good morning. How is Shyam?"

"I called you to talk about that."

She was concerned. "Is he all right?"

"Yeah, nothing to worry about."

"Thank God."

"Listen, *Shyam has moved to USA*."

"What! Why? When?"

"Whoa, whoa, slow down."

"Tell me, please." She was really concerned.

"Two days ago. Took early morning flight to Washington DC."

"You said...*moved*?"

"Yes."

"That sounds...kind of...*permanent*."

"I am not sure but that's what he said...moving..."

"Where in USA, Karan?"

"Sorry, Kaveri, I cannot reveal it. Shyam's instructions."

Kaveri was crestfallen. Tears welled in her eyes.

"I know, Kaveri, I understand."

"No, Karan, you don't know anything..."

"Shyam told me everything that happened between you."

"Yet, you never said anything."

"It's not for me to say or interfere, Kaveri. It's between two adults, who loved each other crazily."

That broke open the floodgates. Kaveri started to sob.

"Easy, Kaveri, easy."

"How can I, Karan, after what I did to him? What all he suffered because of me? I betrayed him, Karan, betrayed his trust and love."

Kaveri sobbed silently for a few moments.

"I have something more to tell you…actually, to *give* you."

She asked him sceptically. "What?"

"Can we meet, Kaveri? I can't do it over phone."

"Sure, we can. Tell me where? Or you could come here."

"Are you free now? I can come in 20."

"Very good. What do you want for breakfast?"

❧✽❧

They settled on a sofa in the drawing room after finishing a breakfast of toast with butter, omelette with grated onions, ginger, and green chillies followed by strong filter coffee.

Karan broached the subject.

"Kaveri, Shyam left these two items with me just before he left; asked me to give them to you *after he left*."

He handed over a large-size cloth-lined envelope and a small leather-lined trinket box.

"What are these, Karan?" She looked perplexed.

"Open and see for yourself."

The small box was very elegant with a leather lining. Kaveri opened it. She found three brass latch keys on a good-looking leather keyring.

She looked at Karan inquiringly.

Karan smiled.

"Keys to *your* apartment, Kaveri."

"What?"

"The apartment that you sold to Karuppayya, the moneylender."

"How are these with you?"

"After you sold it to Karuppayya, Shyam bought it from him at a higher price so that he wouldn't grumble."

She looked at him incredulously.

"It is yours once again, Kaveri. You can move in whenever you wish. All the related documents are in the envelope. Shyam has given it to you, legally. I'll help you complete all the formalities."

Kaveri could not believe her eyes and ears. Tears brimmed in her eyes as she looked at a smiling Karan.

"There is more, Kaveri. Look inside the envelope."

It was a large envelope. Kaveri emptied it on the coffee table. There were the three sets of papers in it. One was a single A4-size sheet neatly folded in half. The second sheaf of papers belonged to the apartment. It contained stamp papers and other official documents. She picked up the third set and casually went through them.

Karan was carefully watching her reaction.

Her hands went to her mouth. "Oh my God!"

Karan could not suppress his smile.

"Something interesting, hunh, Kaveri?"

She looked at him incredulously. Her gaze shifted between the papers and Karan several times.

She held the set of papers in front of Karan's face.

"Shyam has given *Kaveri Kreations* to me. These are the related papers!"

"Yes."

"I don't understand, Karan. I…"

"It's simple, Kaveri. The two sets of documents say that Shyam has given to you the apartment and the fashion designing business."

"But how? I haven't paid even a single rupee to him! He told me that *Kamakshi Finserv* purchased my business. That's all I know. Now, this! Why, Karan?" She was in tears.

"Your tear glands are working overtime." Karan chuckled. "Coming to your question, *don't you know why?*"

She simply kept staring at him.

"I don't want to repeat details of the tragic story. I'll simply say that *Shyam never stopped loving you.*"

"What? He hated me and wreaked vengeance against me. You say he…"

"Yes, I say *Shyam never stopped loving you.* I know. He spoke to me a lot about you and all that happened between you. You thought that he was simply my boss and I his employee! Kaveri, we are good friends. I was with him through the traumatic years after the breakup, not at the time when he was hospitalised and his mother expired, though; after that, when he started *Kamakshi Finserv.* He didn't hide anything from me. I was witness to his devastation, his grief, his multiple losses, his pain, his trauma, his depression. I tried better than my best to lift him up from that dark abyss of depression. I don't know if I was any help there, but, over time, he recovered well and started functioning with newfound determination in his work. He worked ceaselessly in putting *Kamakshi Finserv* among the top organisations; I stood with him in his struggle. But your betrayal – I'm sorry – left such a deep and grievous scar on his mind and heart that even I couldn't placate him. He continued to seethe. That became his driving force – the anger. I was with him throughout his father's illness until he passed. It seemed God Almighty had a grudge against him. I haven't seen another human in my life who can suffer so much and still be so kind to others at the same time. He added a few small ventures to his kitty; then came *Shopping Bag*, a huge venture. He acquired that small, purely local business and turned into a top organisation. I learnt a lot from him."

"He used to be lost in thought for long hours in his wheelchair, even at home. He kept track of your life – I admit I helped him – your marriage, your education, your business venture, your progress, everything. He was a man living within himself, completely withdrawn from the world. He never mixed with anyone except me. We often used to share dinners and sometimes drinks. That's when he used to pour out his heart to me.

"Then, when he felt the time was right, he executed his plan. He was the invisible force that you faced in losing your orders, your contract, your apartment, and, finally, your dream business."

Kaveri was trying to assimilate what she heard.

"Karan, I admit I betrayed him, his love, and his trust. I admit I deserved what he did as revenge. What I did to him had destroyed his life, his family. He lost his mother and father. I loved them, Karan, please believe me. Despite that, I destroyed their family. I was blinded by avarice and never gave a thought to repercussions, to how it might affect him and his family. I was so selfish I never even considered it. I saw a greener pasture; I had to grab it. That was it. He begged me but I wasn't even prepared to talk with him; I just dumped him and walked away. I kept him and his family in the dark about Virendra's alliance lest they should try to talk me out of it. That effectively devastated their lives and I didn't care. The saddest part is I came to know about the deaths of his mother and father only after you sent me to meet him. I stooped to that level. I deserve what I got from him."

She paused to wipe her tears and to catch her breath.

"I am sorry, Kaveri, about how things shaped between you and Shyam. I truly am."

"And now this, Karan, after all that hurt, loss, grief, and anger! Why would he return to me my house and business? Why?"

"I told you, Kaveri. *Shyam never stopped loving you. You were, you are, and you will always be his only love.* When I asked him about it that's what he said. Look, his mission ended when you lost your business. There was nothing more to be done; he told me so. It was never his intension to usurp your business or your apartment. So, he restored them to their rightful owner – *you*. He would never take a rupee from you for that. They were yours. They will always be yours."

Kaveri sobbed covering her face in her palms.

"And I harmed *this man* - my Shyam!"

"There's more, Kaveri. Shyam has also instructed me to transfer some funds to you to restart your life. I'll do it in a couple of days. Be brave. Be strong. You got back your home and business. Forget the past; it can't be erased. In life there's no undo button. Re-establish your home. Restart your *Kaveri Kreations.*

Be busy. Settle down in life. Please do not hesitate to ask me for help in any matter. Okay?"

She nodded.

"What's in the third paper, Karan?"

"I guess it is a letter…from him to you."

"Let me read it, wait…"

"No, you must read it in private, in the solitude of your room. Remember, Shyam is speaking to you through it."

She became very emotional.

"Will I see him again?" Between hiccups.

"Only he can answer that, Kaveri. I shall take leave. Keep in touch. Remember, I will always be there for you…*otherwise I'll have to answer to Shyam!*"

"Will I see *you* again, Karan?"

"I'm just a phone call away, Kaveri."

Karan smiled and got up to leave. Shedding tears, Kaveri ran to him and unabashedly hugged him. Karan consoled her by stroking her back.

☙❀❧

Kaveri stood near the gate looking on as Karan's car drove away.

After Karan left, Kaveri took the documents and keys to her room and bolted the door from inside. She placed the keys and the two sets of stamp papers on the study desk and settled on her bed with Shyam's letter.

She started reading the letter.

Shyam's Letter

"Hi Kaveri,

If you are reading this, it means that Karan has handed over the letter, the documents for your apartment and your business, and the keys to your apartment.

You'd be wondering why I returned the apartment and the business to you after going through all the trouble of taking them away from you. The reason is simple. One thing has nothing to do with the other. Taking away your apartment and business from you had one purpose and one purpose only - teaching you a life-lesson for your betrayal, nothing more. I never wanted to usurp them from you. They were rightfully yours.

I've already narrated in detail what your betrayal did to my life and my family. I lost *everything*. I had to pay you back in the same coin and thus, teach you a lesson. Through the suffering of a few months, you realised the pain of losing something or someone you love dearly. That day in the park, when we were talking, I saw genuine regret in your eyes and tears; they weren't fake. I understood that *you had learnt your lesson*.

Why have I returned your house and business to you? It was never my intension to usurp them but only to make you realise the grave injustice you did to me and my family. That accomplished, I had no need to keep them with me, away from you. So, I restored them to their rightful owner, *you*. I know you are wondering why I haven't taken a single rupee from you towards their cost. The reason is I just couldn't take any money from you because *I loved you*. Also, I have instructed Karan to transfer some funds to you to restart your life. Treat all these as my parting gifts to you, please.

It is sad that things reached this state between you and me. As I see it, *there is no going back from this point*. Well, we both have to live with it.

Concluding, I just want to say this, *I never stopped loving you. You were, you are, and you will be my only love forever*. There's no place for anyone else in my heart and life. Things became this bad between us because of our *karma; it always comes back.*

You may not see me or hear from me ever again but who am I to say that. We cannot know what is in store for us in the future, just like I never could have imagined the breakup or the events that followed. Let us keep doing good *karma* so that, at least in future, neither of us shall be subjected to such trauma.

Be good. Be safe. Best wishes for a happy life.

Good bye, Kaveri.

Shyam"

೧❋೧

Kaveri wept.

೧❋೧

Kaveri's Journal - Final Entry

That was my story. Despite initially being a true-love story, it ended up as a saga of betrayal, hatred, distrust, vendetta, and irretrievable loss of near and dear.

What I did to my Shyam was unpardonable. I realise now that *karma always comes back; it did in my case with vicious force.* I deserved everything that happened to me; no regrets there.

My greatest regret is that I destroyed the love of my life. Yet, Shyam returned to me part of my life – my home and my business, but not himself. That's what he is, has always been, a good human.

Life doesn't always give you a second chance. One has to work for it; I realise that. Shyam has left not only me but also the country to alien shores. Is it because of me? Is it permanent? I am hopeful about what he said in his letter, *'We cannot know what is in store for us in the future'*. Lot of bad has happened. *Maybe there is some good round the corner! May be there is reunion of ravaged souls in the future!* I will work towards that goal – the goal of my life from now on, however long it may take.

I love you, Shyam, I always have.

I hope. I pray.

I got up from the edge of the waters of the Bay of Bengal. I dusted my dress and began my lonely trudge on the sands of Marina beach towards the car park.

Epilogue

Well, life served me paradise on a silver platter and, through my bad *karma,* I let it slip through my avaricious fingers.

I have all the answers now.

I am Kaveri and this was my story, *a sad story of how paradise was lost.*

Other titles by the author

DANCE OF LIFE

THE KIDNAP

EMBERS OF THE PYRE

MISOGYNIST INTERRUPTED

RACE WITH TERROR

LIVING PAGES (Vol. I)
(A collection of short stories)

HEARTFELT (Vol. I)
(A collection of English poems)

ZINDAGI RANG BIRANGI (Vol. I)
(A collection of Hindi poems)

VISHWASGHAT

www.ingramcontent.com/pod-product-compliance
Lightning Source LLC
Chambersburg PA
CBHW031447150726
47990CB00007B/2650